YIAYIA VISITS AMALIA

To my Yiayias, Marietta and Marika, who lived far away from me when I was growing up, and to my granddaughter Amalia, whom I miss until we are together

—mgm

Published by CreateSpace
7290 Investment Drive Suite B
North Charleston, SC 29418

Library of Congress Cataloging-in-Publication Data
Mackavey, Maria, Yiayia Visits Amalia

ISBN-13: 978-1515121862 (CreateSpace-Assigned)
ISBN-10: 1515121860
BISAC: Juvenile Fiction / Transportation / General

YIAYIA VISITS AMALIA

MARIA G. MACKAVEY

ILLUSTRATED BY BEE JOHNSON

Yiayia stood gazing out of her kitchen window. An iris blue sky sat on sparkling snow piled up along the driveway.

"Ah, here comes Tracy," Yiayia whispered to Micah, who stood beside her wagging his tail.

"Hello, Tracy!"
said Yiayia.

"Hello!" smiled Tracy,
patting Micah as he
jumped up to greet her.

Yiayia handed Tracy some
last minute instructions as
she put on her coat and scarf.

"See you in two days!" Yiayia said cheerfully.
She waved goodbye and headed for her car.

Yiayia was on her way to visit her granddaughter Amalia.

Amalia lived in an apartment
in another city with her Mommy
and Daddy.

The road was packed with cars, buses, and trucks of all sizes and colors. Yiayia squeezed between a dump truck and a yellow school bus.

"Everything is moving so slowly," she sighed. She looked at the clock while tapping her fingers on the steering wheel.

Yiayia took the next exit and parked her car outside of the train station. She hurried inside and walked up to the ticket counter.

"Hello," said the lady behind the ticket counter. "Can I help you?"

"I would like a round-trip ticket to Penn Station, please," Yiayia replied, a bit out of breath.

"Just in time!" said the lady as she handed Yiayia her ticket. "Have a good trip!"

TICKETS

Yiayia could hear the train pulling into the station.

"Thank you!" she called back as she ran up the stairs to the platform.

"All aboard!" a voice over the speaker called out.

"Mind your step," the conductor said as Yiayia walked through the open door onto the train.

She looked around and spotted an empty seat next to a window. She plopped down and let out a sigh of relief.

"I made it," she smiled to herself.

Yiayia settled back into her seat as the train pulled out of the station. Fields and houses and cars passed by.

The train rocked gently as it ran along the rails.

It reminded Yiayia of one of Amalia's favorite songs:
The wheels on the bus go round and round...

Yiayia reached for her phone to look at pictures she had taken of Amalia in the past. There was one of Amalia digging sand by the sea, one of Amalia sitting on her daddy's shoulders, and another in her mommy's arms at her Dol Janchi, a traditional Korean first birthday party.

Yiayia put away her phone.
Her eye lids began to close as
her head dropped forward.

She had fallen asleep.

PENN STATION

"Penn Station! End of the line! Be sure to take all of your belongings," said the voice over the speaker. Yiayia opened her eyes and yawned.

She stepped off the train and was swallowed up in a crowd of people rushing in every direction.

Yiayia took the escalator up to the big doors
leading out of the train station.

She walked to the curb and put her hand out to wave for a yellow taxi. Four yellow taxis drove by without stopping. Snowflakes drifted down between the tall gray buildings. Yiayia shivered.

Finally, a yellow taxi cab pulled up to the curb. Yiayia reached down to pick up her suitcase—but it wasn't there!

"Oh no!" Yiayia cried aloud. "I forgot my suitcase on the train!"

She ran back into the train station and hurried down the escalator. Once again, the crowds swirled around her. She stopped in front of a very tall man in a red uniform.

"Excuse me," she said. "I forgot my suitcase on the train. Can you please help me find it?"

"Follow me," the tall man in the red uniform said.

The man led Yiayia through a long line of people with suitcases and bags waiting for their train until they arrived at a desk with a large sign that read, "LOST LUGGAGE CLAIM."

"Hello," the lady behind the counter said. "What color was the suitcase you lost?"

"Blue!" answered Yiayia.

The woman disappeared through a door for a moment.

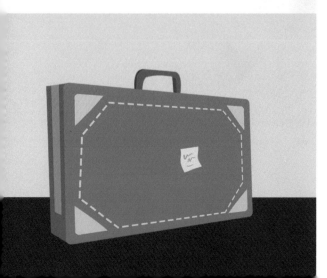

"Is this your suitcase?" the lady asked, pulling out a small blue bag in the shape of a circle.

"No!" said Yiayia. "That's much too round."

"Hmmm." The lady paused. "Is this your suitcase?" She pulled out a giant blue duffle bag.

"No!" said Yiayia. "That's much too big!" She was beginning to worry.

The lady bent down for a minute and then popped back up with a smile.

"Is this your suitcase?" she asked.

"Yes, yes!" cried Yiayia. "That's it! Thank you!"

Yiayia looked down at her suitcase and noticed a yellow post-it stuck on the front.

"How very kind," Yiayia thought to herself.

Someone on the train had found her suitcase and carried it to the Lost Baggage Claim desk. She smiled and headed back out of the station.

Just as she reached the curb outside the train station,
a yellow taxi pulled up.

Yiayia climbed into the taxi and told the driver where she
wanted to go. She sank back into her seat and buckled
her seatbelt. "At last," she thought, "I'm on the way to Amalia!"

The taxi crept along slowly as people spilled onto the
sidewalks and street.

Finally, the taxi turned onto Amalia's street and stopped in front of her building. There at the window, two stories up, was Amalia's face pressed against the window pane. Yiayia happily waved, and Amalia waved back.

Yiayia walked inside the building, through the lobby, and into the elevator. She pressed the button with the number 2 on it and watched as the doors closed in front of her.

Up went the elevator. When it reached the second floor, the elevator stopped, and the doors opened.

Yiayia walked quickly down the long hallway and stopped in front of Amalia's apartment door.

Just as she lifted her hand to reach for the knocker, the door swung open.

"Yiayia! Yiayia!" Amalia cried. Yiayia dropped her suitcase and opened her arms to pick up Amalia, who wrapped herself tightly around Yiayia's neck.

"Love you, Yiayia," Amalia murmured as she felt her grandmother's arms fold snugly around her.